W9-BOM-927

*J*

To my wonderful friends – JC
To Hannah and Jacob – JG

## Crabtree Publishing Company
www.crabtreebooks.com

PMB 16A, 350 Fifth Avenue,
Suite 3308,
New York, NY
10118

612 Welland Avenue,
St. Catharines,
Ontario, Canada
L2M 5V6

Published by Crabtree Publishing Company in 2004
Published in 2002 by Random House Children's Books and Red Fox

Cataloging-in-Publication data

Clarke, Jane.
   Only tadpoles have tales / written by Jane Clarke ; illustrated by
Jane Gray.
      p. cm. – (Flying foxes)
Summary: Kicky the tadpole learns about life in the pond the hard
way but makes a few friends along the way.
   ISBN 0-7787-1484-5 (RLB) – ISBN 0-7787-1530-2 (PB)
   [1. Nature–Fiction. 2. Friendship–Fiction.] I. Gray, Jane -
ill. II. Title. III. Series.

2003022717
LC

Text copyright © Jane Clarke 2002
Illustrations copyright © Jane Gray 2002

The right of Jane Clarke and Jane Gray to be identified as the author and
illustrator of this work has been asserted in accordance with the
Copyright, Designs and Patents Act, 1988.

Set in Cheltenham Book Infant

1 2 3 4 5 6 7 8 9 0  Printed and bound in Malaysia by Tien Wah Press  0 9 8 7 6 5 4 3

NOV – – 2004

# Only Tadpoles Have Tails

Jane Clarke
Jane Gray

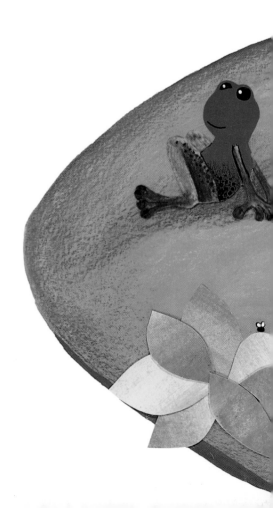

The rainforest frogs were sunning themselves on a giant water lily pad.

"Hoppy," said Kicky to his friend, "when will my tail drop off?"

"In its own good time," Hoppy said.

Why do I still have a tail?

"But you have lost your tail already,"
Kicky said. "And so has everyone else."

I wish my tail
would drop
off now.

"Some tails take a little longer than others," said Hoppy.

"I wish my tail would drop off soon," Kicky said. "Only tadpoles have tails."

"Come on, everybody," said Croaker, who was the biggest. "Let's play leapfrog."

Kicky joined the line. Croaker leaped over Hoppy, Ribbit, and Chirrup, but when he tried to leap over Kicky, he landed flat on his face.

"Ow!" yelled Croaker. "I fell over your stupid tail!"

"Sorry, Croaker,"
Kicky said.

He tried to be careful, but it was no good. His tail got in the way. When it was his turn to jump, his tail hit Croaker in the eye.

**Thwack!**

"Stupid tail!" said Kicky.

"You can't play leapfrog," grumbled Croaker. "You're not a frog. You're a tadpole. Only tadpoles have tails."

"It's not Kicky's fault that he still has a tail," Hoppy said. "Give him another chance."

"All right," said Croaker. "We'll play frogball. Kicky, you go in goal."
"Great!" said Kicky. "I've always wanted to be a goal leaper."

Croaker kicked the ball
as hard as he could.

"What a save!" yelled
Ribbit.

"It's not fair," Croaker said.
"Kicky stopped it with his tail.
Tails are not allowed in frogball.
Only tadpoles have tails."

"I'm very sorry," said
Kicky. "I won't use
my tail again. I
promise."

"You can't be a goal leaper until you've lost your tail," Croaker said.

Kicky was very sad. He jumped into the water and swam off toward a lily pad.

"Can't you do froggy paddle yet?" Croaker laughed. "You swim like a tadpole. Only tadpoles have tails."

Hoppy hopped over to Kicky's lily pad.

"Take no notice of him," she said.
"We all had tails once, even Croaker. You
are a frog, even if you still have a tail."

"I wish I could get rid of my tail,"
sighed Kicky.

"Is it loose yet?" asked Hoppy.
Kicky wriggled his tail.

"I'm not sure. What do you think?"

I hate
my tail!

Hoppy tugged on Kicky's tail.
"I think it might be a bit loose,"
she said.

"I'll call the others . . . Ribbit!
Chirrup! Come and help! And you,
Croaker! You help too!"

Who, me?

PULL!

22

Ribbit, Chirrup, Hoppy, and Croaker
pulled and pulled and pulled, but
Kicky's tail did not come off.

"It's no good," said Kicky sadly. "I'm
not a frog. I'm a tadpole. Only
tadpoles have tails."

"What we need," said Croaker, "is more power. Let's use that branch to make a catapult."

Hoppy, Chirrup, and Ribbit bent the branch down toward the river. Croaker tied Kicky's tail onto it with creepers.

"Hang on a minute!" Croaker shouted. "My foot is tangled up!"

The others were not listening. They let go of the branch.

Wheeeeeeee!

Kicky and Croaker flew
through the air.

They landed in the middle of
the river.

"I've still got my tail," Kicky said.

"Stupid tail!" spluttered Croaker.

"Watch out! Watch out!" cried Hoppy,
Chirrup, and Ribbit, jumping up and down
on the water lily pad. **"Behind you!"**
Kicky and Croaker turned and saw . . .

# PIRANHAS!

"Swim for your life!" Croaker yelled.

With a flick of his tail, Kicky shot off toward the lily pads.

"**Wait!** I can't swim as fast as you!" Croaker gasped. "I don't have a tail!"

That frog swims like a fish.

35

"Keep going!" Kicky called to Croaker.

He turned and cut back in front of the school of piranhas. "Can't get me!" he shouted.

The piranhas turned and grinned vicious grins. Kicky glanced over his shoulder. Croaker had made it to the lily pad.

"Over here, Kicky!" Croaker shouted.

"Quick! They're catching up! Hurry up!
Hurry up!"

Kicky swam faster.

Croaker leaned over the edge of the lily pad to help him. "Quick, Kicky, get out!"

Kicky gave one last flick of his tail and shot out of the water.

SNAP! The piranhas' sharp teeth flashed in the sunlight.

Snap!

Get out of the water!

Kicky sat panting on the lily pad.

"You saved me, Kicky!" Croaker said. "I'll never make fun of your tail again!"

"What tail?" said Kicky. "It's gone! I don't have a tail any more. I'm a frog!"

"Only tadpoles have tails!"

Piranhas and tree frogs like Kicky live in the rainforest. Make a **hungry** piranha like the ones in the story.

YOU WILL NEED:
a piece of cardboard, scissors, colored pencils, and a paper fastener

1. Trace a fish like the one at the bottom of the page on a piece of cardboard and cut it out.

2. Using the left over cardboard, trace a shape like this for the mouth.

Cut here

Stick fastener through this hole.

3. Attach the mouth to the fish shape with the paper fastener.

Paper fastener

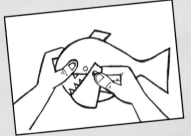

4. Draw the teeth, eyes, and fins, and color it all in.

Piranhas are deadly hunters that can eat small animals in minutes!

In the story, Kicky really wants his tail to drop off. In fact, frogs' tails shrink as the frogs grow up.
Here's how:

Frogs eat me for dinner!

**1.** A female tree frog lays her eggs in a ball of jelly on a tree leaf over water.

Frogs eggs

**6.** The tail is now a short stump. The frog is grown-up and it can eat insects!

**2.** After ten days, the tadpoles hatch and drop into the water. They have gills on the outside so they can breathe in the water.

LIFE CYCLE OF A FROG

Gills

**5.** After twelve weeks, the front legs grow and the tail begins to shrink, just like Kicky's at the beginning of the story.

They eat tiny plants.

**3.** After four weeks, the tadpole grows gills on the inside so it can breathe air outside the water.

**4.** After eight weeks, the tadpole grows back legs.

45

Meet the author:

# Jane Clarke

**How did you get the idea for this story?** We live very close to a lake, and a lot of small frogs come and hop around our garden every spring. I wondered how it must feel to be the last frog to have a tail. When I was a child, I was the last person in my class to lose a front tooth, and I couldn't wait for it to start wobbling. I thought a young frog who still had a tail might feel like that.

**Have you ever met a frog like the ones in the story?** No, even though I lived in Brazil for a while. I have met a lot of ordinary tadpoles and frogs, and I have seen frogs like the ones in the story in a zoo. They are so beautiful, it's hard to believe they are real.

**What kinds of animals do you like?** I like my two dogs, Amber and Bramble, and I am very fond of guinea pigs.

**As a child, what did you wish you could do that you couldn't?** I wished I could roller skate standing on one leg, but I always fell over.

**What animal would you most like to meet?** I'd like to meet a duck-billed platypus.

# Jane Gray

Meet the illustrator.

**What did you use to paint the pictures in this book?** I used acrylic paints. I like the bright colors you can get with them.

**Have you ever met a frog like the ones in the story?** Our garden pond is full of frogs and they all come out and sit on the grass when it rains. They're only common garden frogs though, not colorful rainforest frogs like the ones in the story.

**What kinds of animals do you like?** My favorite animals are cats. I have a cat called Smartie. She's always dashing around and I have to watch out that she doesn't knock over my water when I'm painting.

**Did you draw when you were a child?** I was always drawing from a very early age. My mom is very creative and always encouraged me.

**What gives you good ideas?** I look at what's going on around me. I like to doodle and write my ideas down in a little sketchbook that I always carry with me.

Will you try and write or draw a story?

**Can I be an illustrator like you?** Yes, just keep practicing and draw all the time.

Let your ideas take flight with

# Flying Foxes

### Digging for Dinosaurs
by Judy Waite and Garry Parsons

### Only Tadpoles Have Tails
by Jane Clarke and Jane Gray

### The Magic Backpack
by Julia Jarman and Adriano Gon

### Slow Magic
by Pippa Goodhart and John Kelly

### Sherman Swaps Shells
by Jane Clarke and Ant Parker

### That's Not Right!
by Alan Durant and Katharine McEwen